# Table of Contents

*For Malika the Mischievous*

Marie-Danielle Croteau

# Fred's Halloween Adventure

Illustrated by Bruno St. Aubin
Translated by Sarah Cummins

**First Novels**

Formac Publishing Company Limited
Halifax
2002

Formac Publishing Company Limited acknowledges the support
of the Cultural Affairs Section, Nova Scotia Department of
Tourism and Culture. We acknowledge the financial support of the
Government of Canada through the Book Publishing Industry
Development Program (BPIDP) for our publishing activities.

We acknowledge the support of the Canada Council for the Arts
for our publishing program.

---

**National Library of Canada Cataloguing in Publication Data**

Croteau, Marie-Danielle, 1953-
[Des citrouilles pour Cendrillon. English]
    Fred's Halloween adventure / Marie-Danielle Croteau;
    illustrated by Bruno St-Aubin.

(First novels; #43)
Translation of: Des citrouilles pour Cendrillon.
ISBN 0-88780-577-9 (hdc.).—ISBN 0-88780-576-0 (pbk.).—

    I. St-Aubin, Bruno II. Title. III. Title : Des citrouilles pour
    Cendrillon. English. IV. Series.

PS8555.R6185D4713 2002      jC843'.54      C2002-903307-1
PZ7

---

Formac Publishing Company Limited
5502 Atlantic Street
Halifax, Nova Scotia B3H 1G4
www.formac.ca

Printed and bound in Canada

Distributed in the United States by:
Orca Book Publishers
P.O. Box 468 Custer, WA
USA 98240-0468

Distributed in the UK by:
Roundabout Books (a division of
Roundhouse Publishing Ltd.)
31 Oakdale Glen, Harrogate,
N Yorkshire. HG1 2YJ

# 1
# A Funny Dream

Last night I had an orange dream. There were no people or animals in this dream, just the colour orange in every imaginable size, shape and form. It talked and moved around like a living being.

The doctor told my mother that the dream was because of the accident, that I was still in a state of shock. I don't think that was the reason. I think I was dreaming about summer.

November always makes me a little sad. It's so rainy! Usually I just sit by the window and wait for the snow to arrive. But this year I can't.

The doctor checked my casts and assured me that I was doing fine. What I wanted to hear was that I was doing well enough that he could take the darn casts off! I want my two legs back, and my right arm. I want to be able to move again!

For two weeks I have been stuck in this white room that smells like a hospital. Not surprisingly—it's in a hospital. If only I could go home! Without my cat Rick, I'm not doing fine at all, no matter what the doctor says.

My mom promised she would bring my favourite photo of Rick and me

tomorrow. In the photo I'm holding Rick in my arms and hugging him tight. On the top of the picture I wrote: "Fred-Rick: inseparable."

She said she'd bring in more recent pictures, too. My favourite one was taken when I thought that I would only be apart from Rick when I had to go to school.

I never figured on this stupid accident.

"Fred, I have a wonderful surprise for you!"

Even with my eyes closed, I recognized the nurse's voice. It must be time for Jell-O, banana mousse or tapioca pudding. I knew the drill—and the menu—by heart.

Not very enthusiastically,

I opened one eye. Who did I see but my grandmother Jackie!

She bent over to give me a kiss, then stopped and drew back.

"My oh my! You really did a good job on yourself!"

She bent over again and deposited a light kiss on my forehead. A minuscule, careful kiss.

"I'm afraid I'll hurt you!"

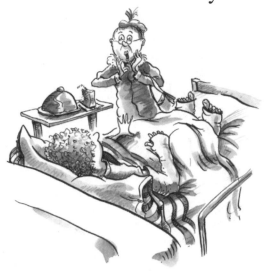

"No worries, Gran! My head is just fine!"

So she gave me a big hug and sat down on the edge of the bed. My granny is so tiny that the mattress didn't sink by even a millimetre.

"I came as quickly as I could, Fred. Unfortunately, I was travelling, as you know. There was no way I could change my return ticket."

"It doesn't matter, Gran. I'm just glad you're here now!"

"So am I! You're not too tired, I hope?"

"Tired?! From lying here in bed all day long?"

"That's good. Because I want you to tell me what happened, and I have a feeling it will take quite a long time."

# 2
# Cinderella's Coach

Remember my friend
William? His father, Jerry
Marshall, has a farm out in
Whippy Corners. That's where
Rick came from.

William invited me to come
spend Halloween weekend
with him.

The invitation came at just
the right time. I was looking
for a refuge for Rick. My
little brother Paul had
smeared him all over with
Mom's hair-removal cream.

Poor Rick! Three-quarters
of his fur came off. He looked

like a newborn mouse!

I couldn't take him anywhere. I was afraid people would make fun of him.

William had promised that we would have a great time. His dad had been elected mayor of Whippy Corners, and since then it had become the pumpkin capital of the province. Halloween was a major celebration there, with a big parade and all kinds of hoopla.

My mom drove Rick and me up there on the Saturday

morning. She helped me carry my suitcase into the house and then left right away, because she always has a lot of work on the weekend.

After she drove off, William and his dad took me behind the barn. A new shed had been built there, with double doors held together by an enormous padlock.

Before opening the doors, Mr. Marshall stopped and looked all around. Was he worried about spies? I also turned and looked around. There was nothing in sight.

Mr. Marshall took off the padlock and bent to whisper something in William's ear. William nodded to show he understood and then went into

the shed. I started to follow him.

"No, no!" cried Mr. Marshall, as if I was about to do something foolish. "Not yet!"

After a couple of seconds, which seemed awfully long to me, William called, "Ready!"

His dad took me by the shoulders and motioned that I could go in. I was intrigued. What extraordinary thing would I find in the shed?

I soon found out.

On a cart with big golden wheels stood the biggest pumpkin in the world! "Planted, tended and harvested by J. Marshall & Son" said the sign that William had just placed prominently on the step.

A 510-kilogram pumpkin! I couldn't believe it.

I leaned back so that I could see the top of the pumpkin and I almost dislocated my neck, it was so high!

I walked all around the colossus, stroking its huge orange belly with my hand. It took me a full five minutes to circle around it.

"What are the wheels for?" I asked.

"What do you think?" William looked at me as if I was a prize idiot.

A light suddenly switched on in my brain. I realized that I was standing in front of Cinderella's coach!

Mr. Marshall was as happy as a kid. He invited me to

climb up a ladder that was placed against the pumpkin. From the top of the ladder I could go down a stepladder inside the pumpkin. William and his dad climbed up on some scaffolding to watch me.

Inside the pumpkin it was as dark and damp as a whale's belly. But I think the pumpkin probably smelled a lot better. It was like being in an organic submarine. Or like being a tiny ladybug inside a gigantic piece of fruit.

"We still have to carve out the windows," said William, noticing that I was beginning to get claustrophobic.

"And install our little princess's throne," added his father.

"We'd better get started soon, Dad. The parade begins in exactly two hours."

"Right you are, son. Karina should be here any minute now."

"Who's Karina?" I asked.

"Cinderella," replied Mr. Marshall. "She's my friend Ilya Barkovitch's daughter."

He had barely finished speaking when we heard the sound of a car in the driveway. Mr. Marshall marshalled us out of the shed and put the padlock back on the doors.

As we walked back to the house, he told me that the pumpkin was going to be the highlight of the parade. No one else knew about it.

"Not even Cinderella?"

"Well, the real Cinderella saw a pumpkin turn into a coach before her very eyes, didn't she? It'll be the same for Karina. She's going to have the surprise of her life!"

Well, it turned out he was wrong. Mr. Marshall would be the one getting a surprise!

# 3
# A Great Disappointment

Ilya Barkovitch was coming down the porch steps when we got to the house.

"Is Karina waiting inside?" asked Mr. Marshall, as he shook the other man's hand.

Mr. Barkovitch shuffled his feet a bit and seemed embarrassed.

"No, she stayed in the car," he finally said.

"Well, what are we waiting for? Tell her to come out here and meet our friend Fred!"

"Well, she's not really presentable..."

Mr. Barkovitch glanced toward the car, and we did too. Karina was inside, watching us miserably. Her face was covered with little red spots.

"She's come down with the chicken pox," her father said. "She woke up this morning covered in spots and running

a raging fever."

"Is it contagious?"

"Not any more. But I'm afraid that she won't be able to be Cinderella in the parade."

Mr. Marshall's smile was gone, and he looked worried. I felt sorry for him, and just as sorry for Karina. She had probably been looking forward to this day with great anticipation.

I ran to get Rick, to try to comfort Karina. Rick was the only cure I knew for every-thing, from boredom to sadness to a bad scrape on your knee. I only had to pick him up and the hurt would go away. I thought it would probably work for Karina, too.

I had wrapped Rick up in a towel to hide his mangy fur. Only his handsome head was visible. Karina reached out and took him in her arms.

Unfortunately, the towel stayed in my hands.

I was so embarrassed! But Karina didn't seem to notice anything. It was as if she didn't see that Rick looked like a sick hyena. She placed him on her lap and began to stroke his head, right between his ears.

Rick started to purr, as happy as a cat can be.

With that, Karina's ugly red spots disappeared. In my eyes, she didn't have chicken pox. She was beautiful, like poor, gentle, unloved Cinderella! Why did she have to get the chicken pox at just the wrong time?

But while I was bemoaning Karina's fate, my own fate

was being decided.

The lively discussion between Mr. Marshall, Mr. Barkovitch and William stopped suddenly, and I felt three pairs of eyes on me. I turned around.

The three conspirators were staring at me in silence, a strange little smile on each face.

"What?" I asked.

"You're our only hope, Fred."

All at once I understood.

"Nooooo!" I protested. "Not that! Don't make me dress up as a girl! You do it, William!"

"William can't. He's the coachman. He's going to drive the team."

"Find someone else!"

"It's too late, Fred. The parade starts in less than two

hours, and we haven't even finished getting the pumpkin ready yet."

"Then let it be a coach without Cinderella!"

"What about all the kids watching? They want to see Cinderella in her coach."

"That's the whole point. They'll just laugh at me. What will I look like, disguised as a girl?"

No way were they going to make me do such a ridiculous thing!

"Well ... all right," sighed Mr. Marshall. He forced a smile.

"Would you like to see Cinderella's coach?" he asked Karina.

She jumped out of the car and came with us to the shed.

This time Mr. Marshall didn't look around for spies. He opened the doors and ushered his guests in. With no pomp and circumstance, he glumly showed them his giant pumpkin. He wasn't happy like a kid anymore.

He had become a grown-up again, a father and a mayor with his own set of worries.

Karina seemed enchanted and yet so sad! I thought she had probably spent hours making herself a dress to wear, just like the real Cinderella.

If only her fairy godmother could appear and make the chicken pox disappear! Unfortunately we weren't living in a fairy tale.

All of these thoughts went

through my mind as I walked back to the house with Karina. We had started back before the others because Karina felt feverish, and I was afraid that Rick was catching a chill and I wanted to take him inside.

Karina didn't come in the house with me. Instead, she went to her father's car. She opened the trunk and took out a big bag, which she brought to the kitchen.

"You know, Fred," she said, handing me the bag. "I believe in magic. If you put this on and go show Mr. Marshall, you'll see that I'm right."

And then she left without a word of explanation.

# 4
# The Hayrick

I stood in front of the mirror. I
looked like a crazy princess.
Or an even crazier prince! At
that moment, there was not a
speck of magic to be found. I
just felt ridiculous, that's all.

I had put on the Cinderella
costume because of Karina.
Her words echoed in my
mind, and I was curious to see
what would happen when Mr.
Marshall saw me.

I didn't want to get Karina's
ballet slippers dirty, so I wore
my boots. You can't imagine
how fabulous they looked

with my dress of white satin and tulle!

I gathered my courage in one hand, my giggles in the other, and took the plunge.

J. Marshall & Son were working in the shed, their backs to the door. They didn't

notice my arrival. I coughed discreetly to catch their attention. William turned first. Mouth agape, he examined me from head to toe and then tugged at his father's sleeve.

Mr. Marshall did not burst out laughing. Instead he stood up and came over and hugged me. He lifted me up and planted a big kiss on my cheek, as noisy as one of my dad's. There were tears in his eyes.

I was extremely embarrassed, but also touched. Now I understood what Karina had meant. There is magic in restoring a little piece of happiness to someone who has lost it.

I had tried on the dress out of curiosity and because Karina had asked me to. And now my fate was sealed. I would be Cinderella.

I couldn't disappoint Mr. Marshall a second time. And Karina was counting on me. Otherwise, why would she have left the dress?

I thought about how she had reached out to take Rick in her arms. She had taught me a good lesson. I had tried to hide Rick because I thought people would laugh at him. But what did I know?

Even if people did laugh, what difference did it make? Rick was still Rick, my own beloved cat.

Even dressed up as Cinderella, I would still be Fred. So I might as well enjoy it! William and his father made a wig for me out of straw. It was the only yellow stuff they could find. When they placed it on my head, we almost died laughing. It looked like what it was: a hayrick. The proof of that came when I turned my back and the horse came up, snatched it off my head and began to eat it. They had to

make me another one.

The time to leave was fast approaching. William put on his coachman's costume and his dad took a picture of the two of us. It was funny!

William and I made a lovely couple, and Rick was the perfect little furry-chinned baby!

At last, William slapped the reins and the coach started moving. It was a five-kilometre trip to the spot where parade participants were supposed to assemble. Five kilometres might not seem like much, but in a conveyance from two centuries ago, it's an enormous distance.

Mr. Marshall drove behind us for a little while. When he saw that everything was going well, he went on ahead. As mayor, he was supposed to start the festivities, so he had to get to town before us.

Rick and I sat beside William on the coachman's bench. Rick was wrapped up snugly and sat purring on my lap.

The coach swayed from

side to side like a boat. The cool autumn air was bracing. The countryside around Whippy Corners smelled great and looked beautiful.

The wide flat fields, bordered by lines of tall pointy trees, had all been plowed in preparation for winter. The furrows looked like parts in a head of auburn hair, and the trees were like green barrettes.

Rick, William and I were enjoying our ride. From time to time, William would crack his whip and the horses would speed up. The giant pumpkin would shift a bit on the cart, reminding us to be careful.

That pumpkin meant a lot to William's father. It was a

way of showing everyone that the future of Whippy Corners lay in pumpkin farming.

That's what Mr. Marshall had told us when he handed the reins over to William. He was counting on us to do him proud.

Whenever the coach started going too fast, William pulled on the reins and the horses slowed down. Everything was going just fine until the last kilometre.

As planned, we stopped briefly so I could get inside the coach. We started off again. Minutes later, an unexpected obstacle appeared—and that's when our troubles began.

# 5
## Runaway Coach

Mr. Marshall had carved several windows in the pumpkin. There was a little one in the front, so I could see William and talk to him. There was another little one in the back, so I could see the road behind us. And there was a window on each door, so the parade watchers could see Cinderella.

The doors themselves were only drawn on. They didn't open, so I couldn't get out that way. Real doors would have weakened the sides of the enormous vegetable and it would have collapsed. I had come in through the top using a cable system Mr. Marshall had built.

I felt like a prisoner in the pumpkin, but I didn't mind. Mr. Marshall had done everything he could to make my incarceration enjoyable.

There was lots of candy and chips and pop, and even a chamber pot, just in case...

All I had to do during the parade was lean out the window, wave and throw packages of roasted pumpkin seeds to the kids along the parade route. Not too difficult!

A few minutes after I had climbed into the pumpkin, a car appeared behind us. It was a long black limousine with tinted windows.

The limousine pulled up beside us in the middle of the road. There were three men in the back seat, gesticulating at us. William smiled and waved back at our admirers.

They continued to gesticulate. They wanted us to stop.

Time was short, and we didn't want to be late. William tapped his watch to indicate that we were in a hurry.

I stayed out of sight and observed the scene. I liked playing Mata Hari. Or rather, James Bond—just because I was dressed as Cinderella didn't mean I was a female spy!

The driver became impatient and honked loudly.

Then the car alarm began to shriek. The noise was unbearable. The horses got scared and began to gallop furiously. This was just at the point where the road begins to go downhill in a long steep slope.

William couldn't stop the horses. He pulled on the reins

and cried, "Whoa, baby! Whoa!" as his father had taught him, but to no avail. The horses were off to the races.

Inside the pumpkin it felt like a space shuttle at blastoff. At least, that is what I imagine it would be like. My pulpy pumpkin shell of a space capsule rocked wildly in all directions. The faster the horses raced downhill, the more I was tossed about.

If William couldn't find some way to slow down the horses, the pumpkin would come off its metal frame. After all, it was only set about 15 centimetres into the frame. No one had expected the coach to be in a speed trial!

Everything was moving so fast, I didn't even have time to be afraid. At least not for Rick or myself. But I was worried about William. I was afraid he would be ejected from his seat.

I tried to help as best I could, and I yelled, "Whoa, baby! Whoa!" along with William. The passengers in the limousine were yelling too, which only made matters worse.

William told me what happened next, after I came to.

Suddenly, William noticed the cart felt lighter. He glanced quickly behind him, and what did he see? The pumpkin was about to pass him.

I was crouched against one wall, and Rick was clinging to

me for dear life. We must have looked like a dishtowel in a dryer, tossed and tumbled up and down and side to side.

If we had been at a point where the road rose gently, the pumpkin would probably have rolled to a stop. But that's not what happened.

Delighted to be released from its moorings, the pump-kin bolted for freedom. It kept on rolling and rolling, faster and faster down the hill.

It was terrifying inside the pumpkin. I just prayed for it to end. For a second, I felt as if I was about to throw up— and then, nothing.

Somehow, William had managed to stop the horse. From the seat of the cart, he

watched the pumpkin barrel on straight toward a pylon, collide with the metal pillar and explode.

He jumped from the cart and ran headlong toward me, followed by the men in the limousine.

They found me lying on the ground, unconscious. I had been thrown from the pumpkin, along with its lid, and I had crashed into the pillar. If it hadn't been for that, I would have probably escaped with only a few bruises.

# 6
## Welcome to the Movies

When I woke up, I was lying in a hospital bed and I hurt all over. My parents were there with my little brother, their eyes welling with tears. William was there too, with his father and a strange man with glasses and a moustache.

"Where's Rick?" I murmured woozily. My jaws felt like papier-mâché.

"Safe and sound," said William. "We took him to your house."

That made me feel better already.

"Do I have anything broken?" I asked.

"Two legs, one arm and your pelvis," my mother said tearfully.

"What about the pumpkin?"

"It's now pumpkin purée," Mr. Marshall joked. "But that doesn't matter. The important thing is that you're alive."

"I feel so bad!" William said, in a strangled voice.

"It's not your fault," the guy with glasses broke in. "It's my fault completely. I wasn't thinking. I was obsessed by my film. I should never have told the driver to honk the horn."

I had no idea what he was talking about. I asked for my own glasses, thinking they would help me see more clearly. My mom placed some kind of jerry-rigged assemblage of twisted earpieces and scratched lenses onto my nose.

"I'm sorry, honey," she said. "The new ones will be ready tomorrow."

"I'm a movie producer," Mr. Moustache went on. "I was scouting locations when I came upon this extraordinary horse-drawn pumpkin. Exactly like a carriage from the 1800s."

He had been delighted. It was just what he needed for a film he was going to make, a parody of a western, starring two famous comics.

The film crew had come to check out Whippy Corners

because it was famous.

"Whippy Corners is famous?" I asked feebly.

"Because of its great pumpkin cultivation. Didn't you know?"

I turned my head toward Mr. Marshall and gave him the best smile I could under the circumstances. I was not only battered and bruised, but broken-hearted, too. Mr. Marshall had lost his chance to get into *The Guinness Book of Records*.

"Don't fret, Fred," he said. "You win some, you lose some."

"If it's any comfort to you, Fred," added the producer, "I can tell you that this story has a happy ending for your friends here."

"How's that?"

"We have decided to rent Mr. Marshall's farm for our film."

"We're going to grow another giant pumpkin," said William.

"Which will be turned into a coach that will be driven by our comic duo," said the producer. "Your friend and his father will teach them how to drive it. You, Fred, are welcome to come to the film set whenever you want. After all, you have already invested quite a lot in the production."

He had an embarrassed little smile on his face. He promised my parents he would pay for all expenses not covered by our health

insurance, like my new
glasses.

I asked him if he could find

me a couple of legs and an arm on short notice. Maybe in his props department.

That made him blush. He looked just like a pumpkin in the setting sun.

# 7
## Time to Get Going

Granny Jackie listened to my story, spellbound.

Then she got up and went over to the window. The days are short in November, and it was already dark. From my bed, I couldn't see anything outside, just the reflection of streetlights on the glass.

"What about Karina?" asked Jackie. "Has she come to visit you?"

"She's going to come next week. William brought me a little note from her."

"You'll have to tell her to

come visit you at home. Not in the hospital."

"Gran, you know I can't leave the hospital yet. Mom would have to look after me full-time. That's not possible, with Paul. And she has to help Dad out in the fish shop."

"Well, Fred, this kind of situation is just what grand-mothers are for."

"You mean you'll stay?"

"As long as you need me."

"So I can go home and see Rick soon?"

"The day after tomorrow."

I was so happy I didn't know what to say. *Thank you* just didn't seem like enough.

"I love you, Gran."

She bent and kissed me on the nose.

Then she started shifting the furniture around. She pushed the two chairs and the little table away from the window.

What had come over her? You never know what to expect with Jackie.

Once she was done with that, she started on the bed. It was on casters, so it was easy to push. She told me to close my eyes and pushed the bed

over to the window. Then she told me to open my eyes again.

I looked outside. It was snowing!

# Three more new novels in the *First Novels Series*!

## Dear Old Dumpling
*By Gilles Gauthier*
*Illustrated by Pierre-André Derome*

Dumpling is very young, just having celebrated his first birthday, and he needs some help growing up. Carl and Gary cannot understand why their dog has gone a little crazy, barking at everything. Carl's mother thinks he might be in love, so the boys and their dog set off around the neighbourhood so that young Dumpling can find his true love!

## Maddie's Millionaire Dreams
*By Louise Leblanc*
*Illustrated by Marie-Louise Gay*

Maddie needs some money, enough money to live like a millionaire. Nicholas has a plan to get lottery tickets at his family's grocery store if she will give him the money. The gang soon find out that the lottery can be addictive. They are losing more than they are winning and now Nicholas has to repay money he has taken from the store. That's when Maddie turns her hand to business to help Nicholas and herself.

# Marilou Cries Wolf

*By Raymond Plante*
*Illustrated by Marie Claude Favreau*

Marilou is bored. Her friends are busy and there's nothing interesting on television. Her dad is repairing an antique radio, so she plays a trick on Boris and then another one on the twins. The police and the fire department arrive to put out a non-existent fire. No one is amused. So they play a trick on Marilou so that she will never, ever cry wolf again.

**Formac Publishing Company Limited**
5502 Atlantic Street, Halifax, Nova Scotia B3H 1G4
Orders: 1-800-565-1975 Fax: (902) 425-0166
www.formac.ca

Marie-Danielle Croteau / Illustrated by Bruno St. Aubin

# Fred's Halloween Adventure

Fred is spending Halloween with his friend William so they can take part in the town's Pumpkin Festival. William and his dad have secretly grown a huge pumpkin, so big that it takes two horses to pull it.

Fred can't wait for the parade to start — until he learns he'll be riding inside the monster vegetable. When the horses start trotting down hill, Fred and the pumpkin are in for a big surprise.

*MARIE-DANIELLE CROTEAU has lived in many parts of the world, including Africa, France and the Antilles. She has written books for people of all ages. This is her sixth book about in this series about Fred and his cat.*
*BRUNO ST. AUBIN is a graphic designer and illustrator, as well as a puppeteer.*

Formac Publishing Company Limited

0-88780-576-0 paper
0-88780-577-9 boards

$5.95 Canada / $3.99 U.S./ £2.99 U.K.

9 780887 805769

First Novels